Written by Craig Robert Carey
Illustrated by Isidre Mones
and Ivan Vazquez

Run Wild

SCHOLASTIC INC.

New York   Toronto   London   Auckland   Sydney
Mexico City   New Delhi   Hong Kong   Buenos Aires

HASBRO and its logo and TONKA are trademarks of Hasbro and are used with permission.
© 2005 Hasbro. All Rights Reserved.

Published by Scholastic Inc.
SCHOLASTIC and associated logos are trademarks and/or registered trademarks of Scholastic Inc.

ISBN 0-439-74681-7

12 11 10 9 8 7 6 5 4 3 2 1   5 6 7 8 9/0

Designed by Maria Stasavage

Printed in the U.S.A.
First printing, October 2005

These vehicles are **WILD**! They all have unusual but important jobs to do.

Deep-sea **submarines** can sail silently and secretly underwater. Some of these vehicles can travel more than 5,000 feet deep!

Another vehicle that goes deep is a **mining dump truck**. It travels far underground to remove rocks, dirt, coal, and other materials, and brings them back to the surface.

The **hydrofoil** uses its water wings to lift its hull above the waves so it can zoom faster and more smoothly. Bigger hydrofoils are used as ferries across choppy channels.

Tonka

Sport hydrofoils can reach speeds greater than 130 miles per hour. Because hydrofoils flip over easily, racing them is widely known as the most dangerous of all sports.

The crusher travels on its tracks wherever it is needed. It's an environmentally friendly vehicle, too, because it helps recycle material, like concrete.

The **cable car** doesn't have a gasoline engine or use electricity like most trains and buses.

It's powered by a moving cable that lies between the rails, beneath the street. The car attaches to the cable with a vice clamp and gets pulled up the steep hills!

Sometimes the only way to cross shallow swamps or frozen lakes is on an **airboat**. Airboats use a big fan to propel themselves forward.

They can reach speeds faster than 135 miles per hour on calm water. Most airboats don't have brakes, so hold on tight!

When a pipeline must be built across long stretches of land, a **pipelayer** is used.

This special vehicle puts huge pieces of pipe right where they're needed to extend the line.

Some pipelayers can lift and place pipes that weigh more than 200,000 pounds!

Instead of putting things down, the **forwarder** picks them up! It's often used to lift the enormous logs that lumberjacks cut down.

The forwarder stacks the logs in its trailer. Then it heads out of the dense forest so the big trucks can carry the logs away on a road.

When a plane needs help from the fire department, the **ARFF truck** is sent in. ARFF stands for Aircraft Rescue and Fire Fighting.

Many ARFF trucks have eight all-terrain wheels so they can travel anywhere. Some of their hose nozzles have a camera on the end so firefighters can see where they're squirting!

When the roads are covered with snow and cars can't get through, it's time for the **snowblower** to get to work!

Some models can move more than 10 million pounds of snow per hour — very useful for clearing airport runways quickly so planes can land!